THE NIGHT KINGS AND NIGHT HEIRS

Hard Cover ISBN 13: 978-1-5154-5398-7
E-book ISBN 13: 978-1-5154-5399-4

THE NIGHT KINGS AND NIGHT HEIRS

ROGER ZELAZNY
AND WARREN LAPINE

OTHER WORKS BY ROGER ZELAZNY

Lord of Light
Roadmarks
The Last Defender of Camelot
The Dead Man's Brother
Creatures of Light and Darkness
The Magic
Shadows & Reflections
Doorways in the Sand
Manna from Heaven
My Name is Legion
A Night in the Lonesome October
Dilvish the Damned
The Changing Land
Today we Choose Faces
Bridge of Ashes
Home is the Hangman
Kalifriki

Chronicle of Amber
Nine Princes in Amber
The Guns of Avalon
The Hand of Oberon
Sign of the Unicorn
The Courts of Chaos
Blood of Amber
Trumps of Doom
Sign of Chaos
Knight of Shadows
Prince of Chaos
Seven Tales in Amber

NIGHT KINGS

by Roger Zelazny

It began like any other night, but this one had a special feeling to it. The moon came up full and splendid above the skyline, and its light spread like spilled buttermilk among the canyons of the city. The remains of the day's storm exhaled mists which fled wraith-like across the pavements. But it wasn't just the moon and the fog. Something had been building for several weeks now. My sleep had been troubled. And business was too good.

I had been trying unsuccessfully to watch a late movie and drink one entire cup of coffee without its growing cold. But customers kept arriving, browsers lingered and the phone rang regularly. I let my assistant, Vic, handle as much of it as he could but people kept turning up at the counter—never during a commercial.

"Yes, sir? What can I do for you?" I asked a middle-aged man with a slight tic at the left corner of his mouth.

"Do you carry sharpened stakes?" he inquired.

"Yes. Would you prefer the regular or the fire-hardened?"

"The fire-hardened, I guess."

"How many?"

"One. No, better make it two."

"There's a dollar off if you take three."

"Okay, make it three."

"Give you a real good price on a dozen."

"No, three should do it."

"All right."

I stooped and pulled out the carton. Damn. Only two left. I had to pry open another box. At least Vic had kept an eye on the level and brought a second carton up from the stockroom. The boy was learning.

"Anything else?" I asked as I wrapped them.

"Yes," the man said. "I need a good mallet."

"We carry three different kinds, at different prices. The best is a weighted—"

"I'll take the best."

"Very good."

I got him one from beneath the adjacent counter.

"Will this be cash, check, or credit card?"

"Do you take Mastercharge?"

"Yes."

He withdrew his wallet, opened it.

"Oh, I also want a pound of garlic," he said as he withdrew the card and handed it to me.

I called to Vic, who was free just then, to fetch the garlic while I wrote up the order.

"Thank you," the man said several minutes later, as he turned and headed for the door, his parcel beneath his arm.

"Good night, good luck," I said, and sounds of distant traffic reached me as the door opened, grew faint when it closed.

I sighed and picked up my coffee cup. I returned to my seat before the television set. Shit. A dental adhesive commercial had just come on. I waited it out, and then there was Betty Davis . . . Moments later, I heard a throat-clearing sound at my back. Turning, I beheld a tall, dark-haired, dark-mustached man in a beige coat. He was scowling.

"What can I do for you?" I asked him.

6

"I need some silver bullets," he said.

"What caliber?"

"Thirty-aught-six. Let me have two boxes."

"Coming up."

When he left I walked back to the john and dumped out my coffee. I refilled the cup with fresh brew from the pot on the counter.

On my way back to the comfortable corner of the shop I was halted by a leather-garbed youth with a pink punk haircut. He stood staring up at the tall, narrow, sealed case high upon the wall.

"Hey Pops, how much is it?" he asked me.

"It's not for sale," I said. "It's strictly a display item."

He dug a massive wad of bills from his side pocket and extended it, his dreamy gaze never leaving the bright thing that hung above.

"I've got to have a magic sword," he said softly.

"Sorry. I can sell you a Tibetan illusion-destroying dagger, but the sword is strictly for looking at here."

He turned suddenly to face me.

"If you should ever change your mind . . . "

"I won't."

He shrugged then and walked away, passing out into the night.

As I rounded the corner into the front of the shop, Vic fixed me with his gaze and covered the mouthpiece of the phone with the palm of his hand.

"Boss," he told me, "this lady says there's a Chinese demon visits her every night and—"

"Tell her to come by and we'll sell her a bedside temple dog."

"Right."

I took a sip of coffee and made my way back toward my chair as Vic finished the conversation and hung up. A small red-haired woman who had been staring into one of the display cases near the front chose that moment to approach me.

"Pardon me," she said. "Do you carry aconite?"

"Yes, I do—" I began, and then I heard the sound—a sharp *thunk*, as if someone had thrown a rock against my back door.

I had a strong feeling as to what it might be.

"Excuse me," I said, "Vic, would you take care of this lady?"

"Sure thing."

Vic came over then, tall and rugged-looking, and she smiled. I turned away and passed through the rear of the shop and into the back room. I unlocked the heavy door that let upon the alley and drew it open. As I suspected, there was no one in sight.

I studied the ground. A bat lay twitching feebly near a puddle. I stopped and touched it lightly.

"Okay," I said. "Okay, I'm here. It's all right."

I went back inside then, leaving the door open. As I headed for the refrigerator I called out, "Leo, I give you permission to enter. This one time. This one room and no farther."

A minute later he staggered in. He wore a dark, shabby suit and his shirtfront was dirty. His hair was windblown and straggly and there was a lump on his forehead. He raised a trembling hand.

"Have you got some?" he asked.

"Yeah, here."

I passed him the bottle I had already opened and he took a long drink, then he slowly seated himself in a chair beside the small table. I went back and closed the door, then sat down across from him with my cup of coffee. I gave him a minute for several more swallows and a chance to collect himself.

"Can't even hit a vein right," he muttered, raising the bottle a final time.

Then he put it down, ran his hands through his hair, rubbed his eyes and fixed me with a baleful gaze.

"I can give you the locations of three who've just moved to town," he said. "What's it worth?"

"Another bottle," I said.

"For three? Hell! I could have brought the information in one at a time and—"

"I don't actively seek out your kind," I told him. "I just provide others with what they need to take care of themselves. I do like having this sort of information, though . . ."

"I need six bottles."

I shook my head.

"Leo, you take that much and you know what'll happen? You won't make it back and—"

"I want six bottles."

"I don't want to give them to you."

He massaged his temples.

"Okay," he said then. "Supposing I had a piece of important information that affected you personally? A really important piece of information?"

"How important?"

"Like life and death."

"Come on, Leo. You know me, but you don't know me that well. There's not much in this world or any other—"

He said the name.

"What?"

He repeated it, but my stomach was already tightening.

"Six bottles," he said.

"Okay. What do you know?"

He looked at the refrigerator. I got up and went to it. I got them out and bagged each one separately. Then I put all of them into a larger brown bag. I brought it over and set it on the floor beside his chair. He didn't even glance downward. He just shook his head. "If I'm going to lose my connection this is the way I want it," he stated.

I nodded.

"Tell me now."

"The Man came to town a couple of weeks ago'" he said. "He's been looking around. He found you. And tonight's the night. You get hit."

9

"Where is he?"

"Right now? I don't know. He's coming, though. He called a meeting. Summoned everyone to All Saints across the river. Told us he was going to take you out and make it safe for us, that this was going to be his territory. Told everyone to get busy and keep you busy."

He glanced at the small barred window high on the rear wall.

"I'd better be going," he said then.

I got up and let him out. I watched him stagger away into the fog.

Tonight might well be the night for him too. Hemoholic. A small percentage of them get that way. One neck is never enough. After a while they get so they can't fly straight, and they start waking up in the wrong coffins. Then one morning they just don't make it back to bed in time. I had a vision of Leo sprawled dessicated on a park bench, brown bag clutched to his chest with bony fingers, the first light of day streaming about him.

I locked the door and returned to the shop. It's a cold world out there.

" . . . horns of the bull for *malocchio*," I heard Vic saying. "That's right. You're welcome. Good-bye."

I kept going, up to the front door. I locked it and switched off the light. I hung the CLOSED sign in the window.

"What is it?" Vic asked me.

"Turn off the phone."

He did.

Then, "Remember when I told you about the old days?" I said.

"Back when you bound the adversary?"

"Yup. And before that."

"Back when he bound you?"

"Yup. You know, one of these days one of us will win—completely."

"What are you getting at?"

"He's free again and he's coming and I think he's very strong. You may leave now if you wish."

"Are you kidding? You trained me. I'll meet him this time."

I shook my head.

"You're not ready. But if anything happens to me . . . If I lose . . . Then the job is yours if you'll have it."

"I told you a long time ago, back when I came to work for you—"

"I know. But you haven't finished your apprenticeship and this is sooner than I'd thought it would be. I have to give you a chance to back out."

"Well, I won't."

"Okay, you've been warned. Go unplug the coffee pot and turn out the lights in back while I close down the register."

The room seemed to brighten a bit after he left and I glanced up. It was an effect of diffused moonlight through a full wall of fog which now pressed against the windows. It hadn't been there moments ago.

I counted the receipts and put the money into the bag. I got out the tape.

There was a pounding on the door just as Vic returned. We both looked in that direction.

It was a very young woman, her long blonde hair stirred by the wind. She had on a light trench coat and she kept looking back over her shoulder as she hammered on the panel and the pane.

"It's an emergency!" she called out. "I see you in there! Please!" We both crossed to the door. I unlocked it and opened it.

"What's the matter?" I asked. She stared at me. She made no effort to enter. Then she shifted her gaze to Vic and she smiled slightly. Her eyes were green and her teeth were perfect.

"You are the proprietor," she said to me.

"I am."

"And this . . . ?"

"My assistant—Vic."

"We didn't know you had an assistant."

"Oh," I said. "And you are . . . ?"

"His assistant," she replied.

"Give me his message."

"I can do better than that," she answered. "I am here to take you to him."

11

She was almost laughing now, and her eyes were harder than I had thought at first. But I had to try.

"You don't have to serve him, " I said.

She sobered suddenly.

"You don't undrstand," she told me. "I have no choice. You don't know what he saved me from. I owe him."

"And he'll have it all back, and more. You can leave him."

"Like I said, I have no choice."

"Yes, you do. You can quit the business right now."

"How?"

I extended my hand and she looked at it.

"Take my hand," I said.

She continued to stare. Then, almost timidly, she raised hers. Slowly, she reached toward mine . . .

Then she laughed and jerked hers back.

"You almost had me there. Hypnosis, wasn't it?"

"No," I said.

"Well, you won't trick me again."

She turned and swept her left arm backward. The fog opened, forming a gleaming tunnel.

"He awaits you at the other end."

"He can wait a moment longer then," I told her, "Vic, stay here."

I turned and walked back through the shop. I halted before the case which hung high upon the wall. For a moment I just stared. I could see it so clearly, shining there in the dark. Then I raised the small metal hammer which hung on the chain beside it and I struck.

The glass shattered. I struck twice again and shards kept falling upon the floor. I let go the hammer. It bounced several times against the wall.

Carefully then I reached inside and wrapped my hand about the hilt. The dreaded familiar feeling flowed through me. How long had it been . . . ?

I withdrew it from the case and held it up before me, my ancient strength returning, filling me once again. I had hoped that the last time would indeed be the last time, but these things have a way of dragging on.

When I returned to the storefront the lady's eyes widened and she drew back a pace.

"All right, Miss," I said. "Lead on."

"Her name is Sabrina," Vic told me.

"Oh? What else have you learned?"

"We will be transported to All Saints Cemetery, across the river."

She smiled at him, then turned toward the tunnel. She stepped into it and I followed her.

It felt like one of those moving walkways the larger airports have.

I could tell that every step I took bore me much farther than a single pace. Sabrina strode resolutely ahead, not looking back. Behind me, I heard Vic cough once, the sound heavily muffled within the gleaming, almost plastic-seeming walls.

There was darkness at the end of the tunnel, and a figure waited, even darker, within it.

There was no fog in the place where we emerged, only clear moonlight from amid a field of stars, strong enough to cause the tombstones and monuments to cast shadows. One of these fell between us, a long line of separating darkness, in the cleared area where we stood.

He had not changed so much as I felt I had. He was still tailer, leaner and better-looking. He motioned Sabrina off to his right. I sent Vic to the side, also. When he grinned his teeth flashed, and he raised his blade—so black as to be almost invisible within its faint outlining nimbus of orange light and he saluted me casually with it.

I returned the gesture.

"I wasn't certain that you would come," he said.

I shrugged.

"One place is as good as another," I replied.

"I make you the same offer I did before," he stated. "to avoid the nastiness. A divided *realm*. It may be the best you can hope for."

"Never," I responded.

He sighed.

"You are stubborn."

"And you are persistent."

"If that's a virtue, I'm sorry. But there it is."

"Where'd you find Sabrina?"

"In the gutter. She has real talent. She's learning fast. I see that you have an apprentice now, also. Do you know what this means?"

"Yes, we're getting old, too old for this sort of nonsense."

"You could retire, brother."

"So could you."

He laughed.

"And we could both stagger off arm in arm to that special Valhalla reserved for the likes of us."

"I could think of worse fates," I said.

"Good, I'm glad to hear that. I think it means you're getting soft."

"I guess we'll be finding out very soon."

A series of small movements caught my gaze, and I looked past him. Dog-like forms and bat-like forms and snake-like forms were arriving and settling and moving into position in a huge encircling mass all around us, like spectators coming into a stadium.

"I take it we're waiting for your audience to be seated," I said, and he smiled again.

"Your audience, too," he replied. "Who knows but that even you may have a few fans out there?"

I smiled back at him.

"It's late," he said softly.

"Long past the chimes of midnight."

"Are they really worth it?" he asked then, a sudden serious look upon his face.

"Yes," I replied.

He laughed.

"Of course you have to say that."

"Of course."

"Let's get on with it."

He raised the blade of darkness high above his head and an unearthly silence poured across the land.

"Ashtaroth, Beelzebub, Asmodeus, Belial, Leviathan . . ." he began.

I raised my own weapon.

"Newton, Descarte, Faraday, Maxwell, Fermi . . ." I said.

"Lucifer Rofocale," he intoned, "Hecate, Behemoth, Put Satanas, Ariaston . . ."

"Da Vinci, Michelangelo, Rodin, Maillol, Moore ... " I continued.

The world seemed to swim about us, and this place was suddenly outside of space and time.

"Mephisto!" he cried out. "Legion! Lilith! Ianoda! Eblis!"

"Homer, Virgil, Dante, Shakespeare, Cervantes," I went on.

He struck and I parried the blow and struck one of my own to be parried in turn myself. He continued his chanting and increased the tempo of his attack. I did the same.

After the first several minutes I could see that we were still fairly evenly matched. That meant it would drag on, and on. I tried some tricks I had almost forgotten I knew. But he remembered. He had a few, too, but something in me recalled them also.

We began to move even faster.

The blows seemed to come from every direction, but my blade was there, ready for them when they fell. His had a way of doing the same thing. It became a dance within a cage of shifting metal, row upon row of glowing eyes staring at us across the field of the dead. Vic and Sabrina stood side by side yet seemed oblivious of each other in their concentration upon the conflict.

I hate to say that it was exhilirating, but it was. Finally, to face once again the embodiment of everything I had fought across the years. To have total victory suddenly lie but a stroke away, if but the right stroke might be found . . .

I redoubled my efforts and actually bore him back several paces. But he recovered quickly and stood his ground then. A sigh rose up from beyond the monuments.

"You can still surprise me," he muttered through clenched teeth, slashing back with a deadly attack of his own. "When will this ever end?"

"How's a legend to know?" I replied, giving ground and striking again.

Our blades fed us the forces we had come to represent and we fought on, and on.

He came close, very close, on several occasions. But each time I was able to spin away at the last moment and counter-attack.

Twice, I thought that I had him and each time he narrowly avoided me and came on with renewed vigor.

He cursed, he laughed, and I probably did the same. The moon dropped down and sparklets of dew became visible upon the grass. The creatures sometimes shifted about, but their eyes never left us. Vic and Sabrina exchanged several whispered conversations without looking at each other.

I swung a head-cut, but he parried and riposted to my chest. I stopped it and tried for his chest, but he parried . . .

A breeze sprang up and the perspiration on my brow seemed suddenly cooler. I slipped once on the damp ground and he failed to take advantage of my imbalance. Was he finally tiring?

I tried pressing him once more, and he seemed a bit slower. Was I now gaining an edge or was it a trick on his part, to lull me?

I nicked his biceps. The barest touch. A scratch. Nothing real in the way of an injury, but I felt my confidence rising. I tried again, mustering all of my speed in a fresh burst of enthusiasm.

A bright line appeared across his shirtfront.

He cursed again and swung wildly. As I parried it I realized that the sky was lightening in the east. That meant I had to hurry. There are rules by which even we are bound.

I spun through my most elaborate attack yet, but he was able to stop it. I tried again, and again. Each time he seemed weaker, and on that last one I had seen a look of pain upon his face. A restlessness came over our gallery then, and I felt that the final sands were about to descend the hourglass.

I struck again, and this time I connected solidly. I felt the edge of my weapon grate against bone as it cut into his left shoulder. He howled and dropped to his knees as I drew back for the death blow.

In the distance a cock crowed, and I heard him laugh.

"Close, brother! Close! But not good enough," he said. "Sabrina! To me! Now!"

She took a step toward him, turned toward Vic, then back to my fallen nemesis. She rushed to him and embraced him as he began to fade.

Aufwiedersehen!" he called to me, and they both were gone.

With a great rustling rush then, like blown leaves, our audience departed, flapping through the sky, flashing along the ground, slithering into holes, as the sun cut its way above the horizon.

I leaned upon my blade. In a little while Vic came up to me.

"Will we ever see them again?" he asked.

"Of course."

I began walking toward what I saw to be the distant gate.

"Now what?" he said.

"I'm going home and get a good day's sleep," I told him. "Might even take a little vacation. Business is going to be slow for a while."

We crossed the hallowed earth and exited onto a sidestreet.

THE NIGHT HEIRS

by Warren Lapine

The full moon rose up over the city, gloriously shining through and reflecting on the mists rising from the pavement, the only remnants of a late afternoon storm. The moon seemed enormous in that illusionary way that it can just upon rising. I would have liked to be able to enjoy the beauty of that magnificent orb, but I knew the portents. My life was about to change and I didn't want it to.

Business was good, entirely too good. I moved away from the cash register to help a slim, young woman who was fingering a wooden stake.

"Can I help you?

She looked up, a thoughtful, far away look in her eyes. "I'm not sure. I really don't know much about this, but I think I need one of these."

"Well, if you need one of those I'd also recommend that you purchase a mallet and some garlic."

"Yes," she said, her mind seemingly a million miles away, "I think I heard or read something about garlic."

"Do they sparkle?" I asked her.

"Excuse me?"

"The person you plan to use this stake on, does he or she sparkle?"

"Now that you mention it, yes I suppose he does sparkle a little bit if you look at him in just the right light."

"Then you'll also want a copy of The Book of Mormon."

"The Book of Mormon?"

I nodded, "I'm not sure why, but it seems to work better than the Bible does on the ones that sparkle."

I got her supplies together and she handed me her credit card. A moment later she walked off into the night, reflected moonlight glinting silver in her long, straight hair.

Since the store was now empty I returned to my office to watch a rerun of Neil DeGrasse Tyson's *Cosmos*. But I'd only just settled into my chair when I heard the bell on the front door chime. I walked back out into the storefront to find three very stout, very short men walking down one of the store's many aisles muttering angrily to one another.

"Can I help you, gentlemen?" All three started as if no one in a store had ever asked them if they could help them before.

"Who are you?" the largest of the three demanded.

"Vic," I said helpfully, "I own the store."

They grumbled a bit more, I thought I might have heard the words "too tall" and "pretty boy" among others. Then the biggest and clearly the leader pointed up at the wall behind me. "How much for that?"

I glanced over my shoulder. High up on the wall in a glass case was a sword gleaming much brighter than it had any right to considering how little light was actually falling upon it. I turned back to my grumpy customers. "I'm afraid that's for display only."

"Name your price," Grumpy growled.

"It's not for sale. Is there something else I could help you gentlemen with?"

A bit more grumbling and then the leader said, "We need provisions for a . . . um . . . we need to outfit for a . . . "

I decided to cut to chase and save us both some time. "Are there thirteen of you or are there seven of you?"

"That's none of your damn business," Grumpy spat at me.

"Fine, suit yourself, you'll excuse me if I don't show you the way out."

Grumpy flew into a rage. "How dare you speak to me like that. Do you know who I am? I am Thor—"

"Look, Thor," I said interrupting what I am certain would have been a marvelous monologue. "It's up to you, I don't care if you want my help or not. If there are seven of you then I'd recommend the Whistle While You Work package of mining tools. If there are thirteen of you then I'd recommend the Misty Mountain package that includes weapons and some dragon repellant."

His anger evaporated. "You have dragon repellant?"

"Guaranteed to repel dragons for up to sixteen hours per application."

"Does it work?" one of Grumpy's friends asked?

"No one has ever come back looking for a refund," I answered, smiling.

Twenty minutes later I was helping the three of them load their gear into a rather anachronistic cart pulled by two ponies and steered by an old man in a funny hat.

As I made my way back into the store the phone began to ring. I reached it on the 4th ring. "This is Vic, can I help you?"

The voice on the other end belonged to a very young girl and she sounded not quite scared, but close. "I hope so. An owl banged into my window tonight. I think it's still breathing, but I'm not really sure. But anyway, it had a message tied onto its right leg. And well, um, there's no way I can get to London in time to buy . . . " The caller's voice trailed off.

"I'm assuming you need some robes, a spell book, a wand, and other assorted things?"

"Yes," she said, brightening. "Do you have them in stock?"

"I do. Just bring your letter here tomorrow and we'll get you all fixed up."

"Wonderful, this is all so I exciting, I can hardly wait."

"Then we'll see you tomorrow, goodnight." I hung up the phone before she could say anything else.

I was happy for the kid, really I was, she was about to start a grand adventure. But right now all I could think about was how my life was about to change; and, that really, no matter how tonight turned out I couldn't imagine that my life was going to be the better for it. When I signed on for this I could never have imagined it playing out this way. But then I guess that's the secret of life: nothing ever goes as planned.

I locked the door and flipped the phone over to voice mail. I needed to think, to clear my mind for what I knew was coming. Really it had all started three years ago when Sabrina had reached out to me.

*

She'd called my cell, I almost never gave that number out so I was very surprised when it rang and I didn't recognize the number calling. "This is Vic, can I help you?"

"Vic, this is Sabrina."

"Sabrina?"

"Yes, you remember, Sabrina from All Saints Cemetery."

"Oh, yes, certainly." It had been twenty-five years since that night in the cemetery, but you don't forget watching the Powers duel, nor do you forget a face as beautiful as Sabrina's.

"This is awkward, I'm calling about your master."

"My master? Oh . . . you mean my boss."

"Right, when was the last time you saw him?"

"I'm not really sure I should be having this conversation with you."

"The last time I saw your boss was when he visited with my master. The two drank three bottles of Chianti and then they just staggered off arm in arm into the night. That was almost four weeks ago and my master hasn't returned since. My sources tell me you've been working the store alone of late."

I paused trying to gather my thoughts. Could this be some kind of a trick? "That sounds about right. Yeah, four weeks."

"Did he say anything to you about where he and my master might be heading?"

"Hell, he didn't even say anything about going to visit your master."

"I'm worried," she said, sounding worried.

"I am too," I confessed.

"Perhaps we should pool our resources and try to find them."

I thought about that for a moment. I was worried about my boss, sure, but could I trust Sabrina? Even if I could, should I? "You could come to the store and we could discuss this if you'd like."

"Your store is awfully public. We have no idea who might be behind these disappearances. I'd rather meet someplace more private. You could come to our place. It's on the edge of the city and it's rather secluded."

I had not realized that the two lived anywhere near the city. "Okay, what's the address?" She gave it to me and I hung up the phone after agreeing to be there in an hour.

I looked up at the sword on the wall and wondered if I should take it with me. This could be a trap. I'd trained long and hard on the uses of the sword. But my boss Sam—not his real name, real names have too much power—had instructed me not to use it unless I was certain that it was needed. He also told me that when the time came I'd be certain. And I wasn't certain what I needed to do, so that ruled out the sword. And really nothing says I trust you like showing up wielding a sword. Still, one likes to take precautions.

I opted for my trusty Colt 45 in a shoulder holster. That necessitated my wearing a light jacket that the weather didn't really call for. Honestly, I wasn't worried about Sabrina or her master trying to set me up. The rules don't work that way. You can't just kill one of the Powers, or their apprentices, in a drive by or with a weapon other than one of the swords. And even if you have one of the swords at your disposal you can only use it when the conditions are correct. Remembering how every fiber of my being vibrated with power during the last duel, I knew the conditions weren't correct. But what if some other player had entered the game? What if someone was hunting both sides? Did they have to play by the same rules we did?

At the appointed hour I found myself driving up a long, winding driveway. The house, really a mansion, was tucked away from the road by a series of rolling hills. Finally the driveway opened out into a wide parking area in front of the well manicured lawn. Just down the hill from the house was a large gazebo overlooking a sprawling ornamental pond. The overall effect was one of enormous wealth. I knew my boss also controlled vast amounts of wealth, but he chose not to display it quite so openly. In fact, he'd been rather put out when I'd purchased the convertible Aston Martin I was now driving.

I parked the car, looked up at the clear sky, and decided not to bother putting the top up. I pushed my sunglasses back onto the bridge of my nose and got out of the car. Gravel crunched under my shoes as I walked to the front door. Sabrina opened it before I got close enough to ring the bell. I hadn't seen her is nearly 25 years. If she'd aged even a day it didn't show. She had a very pretty face framed by long blond hair that seemed to be moving about in a breeze, except that there wasn't one. Her eyes had a hard edge to them, but they were green and beautiful, and I knew that if she smiled her teeth would be very white and quite perfect.

"Thank you for coming," she said, showing me those perfect teeth.

I nodded.

"Please come in," she said moving aside.

I did that thing.

"Can I take your coat?"

I smiled, "Thank you, no it's really quite comfortable."

She smiled back at me and I noticed she was also wearing a light jacket.

She lead me to a bay window with two comfortable chairs and a small coffee table. The window looked out over the ornamental pond I'd seen coming in. There was a pot of tea and two cups on the table. "Can I offer you some jasmine tea?" she asked sitting down.

I took the other chair. "Yes, please," I said, taking off my sun glasses and placing them into the inside pocket of my jacket.

She poured tea into both cups and handed one to me. As I was thanking her she took a sip of hers. Well, that made it clear it wasn't poisoned, so I took a sip of mine. It was very pleasant with just a hint of honeysuckle under the subtle jasmine.

"This is very nice," I offered.

She smiled, but the smile didn't reach her eyes. "So you don't have any idea where our masters are?" she asked, getting right to the point of our visit.

"None. Honestly, I don't think my boss was planning to leave. I've gone through all of our accounts and I can't find any transactions that suggest he planned anything at all."

She seemed to shrink a little into herself. "I've gone though all of ours and came to the same conclusion. My master never went anywhere without plans. If you knew where to look you'd always know when he was planning something. I'd tried to explain to him over and over again that computers leave traces, but he just couldn't understand it."

I chuckled.

She stood up and approached the window, her back to me. I realized right away why she'd done that. A tear had slipped out of the corner of her eye and she hadn't wanted to show me that moment of vulnerability. I'm not sure why I did it, but I stood up and placed my hand on her shoulder, she turned slowly towards me and then I hugged her.

She let me hold her for a long moment and then broke away. She wiped at her tears, which were streaming freely now. "Why did you do that?" she demanded.

"You looked like you needed a hug."

She studied me long and hard. For a moment it almost seemed as though she was reading my mind. "You mean that don't you? You didn't have any ulterior motives at all."

Sabrina might very well be the most beautiful woman I had ever met, and she was certainly my type, but in that moment my only concern had been for her pain. "I didn't," I said barley above a whisper.

And suddenly she was in my arms again. But this time her lips sought out mine and she kissed me with a passion fiercer than any I'd ever experienced before in my long life. There was an awkward moment when we each ran into the other's holstered gun. But her laugh broke the awkwardness and the passion returned.

THE NIGHT KINGS AND NIGHT HEIRS

I spent the night and in the morning we decided to search out our missing mentors together. We went through all the records that they had left behind. In the end we spent three months traveling the world, moving from one place of power to the next. We met with hundreds of people who had had dealings or connections with our missing mentors, but no one had seen or heard from either of them. Looking back on it, those were some of the most glorious days of my life. As much as we were genuinely seeking out our lost mentors we were also getting to know one another. The time was very much like a three month long honeymoon.

Honestly, it was my first real relationship. Sam had always warned me about getting close to anyone. If we loved, the enemy would use that against us. So we could never let ourselves care too much about anyone lest they be used as leverage against us. Of course, falling in love with Sabrina meant not having to worry about the enemy using her against me; she *was* the enemy.

We spent hours amiably debating our positions. I'd tried to get her to switch to my side, but she insisted that she owed it to her master to continue on in his footsteps. She'd tried to get me to defect, pointing out that virtually all of the ills of the day were created by science. Global warming and pollution were the new dark ages, she'd argued, and only magic could put right what science was destroying. In the end neither of us could sway the other, but still our relationship grew stronger and I was almost glad we didn't find either of our missing mentors.

On the night we arrived home I decided it was time to tell Sabrina something I'd come to realize. "Sabrina, I love you."

She had been looking down at something and she looked quickly up at me. "You know that eventually one of us will have to kill the other."

I nodded, "But that doesn't change how I feel for you, and I've never been any good at lying to myself."

She smiled, but the smile didn't make it to her eyes. "You are a wonderful man, and I'm glad that fate has tossed us together as it has, but . . ."

"But?"

"But if I let myself love you, then it might slow my hand when it is time for me to kill you, or once I've killed you it might torment me for eternity that I killed the only person I'd ever loved. I'm not signing on for that."

I resisted the urge to tell her I didn't think she had any chance of killing me in a duel. My father had been a gold medalist in fencing in one of the early Olympics, and I was considerably better with a blade than he had ever thought of being. It was that ability that had attracted Sam's attention to me. And in the more than one hundred years that I'd been in Sam's employ I had studied with scores of sword masters in every style imaginable. Frankly, other than Sam, and perhaps Sabrina's master, I wasn't certain that there had ever been a better swordsman than myself. Still, her master wouldn't have chosen her if he'd thought she had no chance of defending herself.

There's a saying that no swordsman should ever forget: A good big swordsman always beats a good small swordsman. Instead of giving voice to any of these thoughts I said, "Does that mean we're over?" I think a tear might have slipped from my eye.

She laughed, "No, it just means I don't plan to let myself love you. I can't imagine having a relationship with anyone else. How would I explain who I am and what I do to them? No, being with you is as uncomplicated in that department as it could possibly be."

*

That had been three years ago. My love for her had grown deeper than I would have thought possible. She still would not admit to loving me, but I could live with that; she was there and that was all that mattered. But I could feel the power growing around me. It was going to happen tonight. Tonight I would heft the magic blade to defend the powers of science and light and Sabrina would brandish her darker blade for the powers of magic and darkness. There were three ways it could end. One of us could die and that would fix the course of the world for all of eternity. One of us could bind the other and then the course of the world would be set for hundreds of years. Bindings had caused the dark ages and the industrial revolution. Or we could fight to a draw, and that would give us, if the records our mentors left behind were correct, another twenty-five to two hundred and fifty years before the power rose again. There was no way of knowing how long between times.

But really, I'd be lying if I said I had any other concern than how I was going to live without Sabrina. I couldn't sacrifice my own life for her no matter how much I loved her. Not and have mankind fall into an eternal dark age. It was also too risky to try to fight for a draw. If one of us bound the other it would be hundreds of years before we'd have any kind of interaction again. And even if we were fortunate enough to fight to a draw, how could our relationship possibly survive such a life and death conflict. Tonight my life changed forever and damn it, I didn't want it to. I liked my life exactly as it was.

Some indeterminate time later I looked up and there was a wall of fog pressed up against the glass of the shop's door. I hadn't seen it roll in; one moment it hadn't been there and the next it was. I recognized the fog, I'd seen it before. Morosely, I walked over to the case that the sword hung in. I fished a key out of my pocket and unlocked the case. My boss has always kept it in a case that could only be opened by smashing the glass, but as the one who had had to sweep up the glass afterwards, I'd insisted on a cabinet with a very good lock instead.

I reached into the case and took the sword down by the hilt. I'd held the sword in my hands before and each time I had I'd been able to feel its immense power like a strong current just below the surface. This time, however, the power came roaring through the blade and flooded my being. This was strength like nothing I'd ever experienced before. How could anyone or anything hope to stand before it?

Resolutely I walked to the door and opened it. The fog seemed to open up a tunnel for me to follow. I locked the shop's door and walked into the tunnel of fog. As I strode towards what I knew would be my first, if not my last, battlefield it felt as if I were walking on one of those electric walk ways that they have at the larger airports. Each step covered far more ground than a single pace.

When I came to the end of the tunnel I was not surprised to find myself at All Saints Cemetery. There was no fog here. The full moon shown like some cold, Greek goddess that had no care as to which Power might triumph. It was a beautiful symmetry that our first duel should take place where our mentors' final battle had taken place. Tears welled up in my eyes as I looked at Sabrina. The landscape about us was in darkness and shadows, but my blade reflected and multiplied the moonlight, giving me enough light to see all that I needed to see. She was beautiful, with her pale blond hair moving about in a nonexistent breeze. She was dressed all in black, but the blade in her hand was blacker than the darkest void. It seemed to be drawing light into itself.

Aligned behind her were dozens of creatures of darkness scurrying about. They were misshapen and twisted like something out of a very bad horror movie. "We don't have to do this." I said, "You don't owe your master anything now that he's gone."

She smiled that smile, the one that never makes it to her eyes. "No, I cannot betray his memory. But as I recall he offered your master a joint reign. I will offer that to you now, as well."

I'd be lying if I said I hadn't been mightily tempted. Why not try? Why not see if the two of us could entwine science and magic for the good of all mankind? But Sam's words came echoing back through the years to my ears. "The enemy is seductive. But their power corrupts, we cannot allow it to abide."

I shook my head. "No, I can't accept that offer. Tonight we end this." She nodded and then I said the words I'd promised myself I wouldn't. "Sabrina, no matter how this ends, I love you."

She didn't respond to my words as she moved toward me blade swinging faster than I would have thought possible.

"Abaddon, Balberith, Lerajie, Sorath," she intoned."

"Tyson, Sagan, Hawking, Einstein, Curie." I responded.

"Lucifer, Vassago, Rahab, Kunopegos, Ronobe."

"Kant, Kierkegaard, Nietzsche, Aedesia."

THE NIGHT KINGS AND NIGHT HEIRS

The world seemed to bend and fold in upon itself and I knew that we were now locked in a battle outside of space and time.

I had expected to take the battle to Sabrina, but her dark blade seemed to be flashing at me from every direction. My blade parried blow after blow, but she was so fast that I could not even consider trying to riposte for fear that I would miss her next blow.

I have faced fencers that were faster than me before. And in those instances I would wage a defensive fight and wait for them to tire. But Sabrina was so fast that I wondered if I could last that long.

I drew power from my blade as Sam had taught me and decided to try a bat parry. Sabrina's blade came towards me and I knocked it away with every ounce of strength I had while directing my blade to move from the parry directly to her torso. But when my blade reached where she had been standing she wasn't there and I felt a burning along my right bicep.

"Damn," I swore as I realized that she'd scored a hit.

"You can't win," she said. Her words did not bother me nearly as much as the fact that she seemed not to be the least bit winded when she spoke.

"The night is yet young," I replied with a false bravado that I hoped she could not detect. In more than a century as a fencer I had only faced one opponent who was better than me and that had been Sam. But I knew with absolute certainty that Sabrina was my better. I had no hope of defeating her. And yet I had to try. If I somehow escaped this night with my life I would have to redouble my time with a blade in anticipation of our next encounter.

"Where did you learn to fence like that?" I asked trying to distract her.

"In Hell," she said, her blade lunging directly for my heart.

I beat the sword aside and tried to step into her as her momentum pulled her forward. Perhaps I could land a blow to her head with my fist and even my odds. Unchivalrous I know, but this wasn't the Olympics. Again I missed and again I felt a burn as she passed. This time it was my left shoulder. How the Hell could anyone be this good? Neither wound was deep; she didn't dare commit the time it would have taken her to push the blade deeper for fear

30

that my strength might be able to come into play. I could see that her plan was to kill me with a thousand cuts if necessary.

You learn interesting things about yourself when you think you're going to die. I realized I didn't really fear death, but that it still made me angry—angry that I could dedicate more than a hundred years of my life getting ready for a single moment and find myself not good enough when that moment finally arrived.

I fought with everything I had, but Sabrina never once broke tempo. She was never in danger of my going on the offensive. Unless she made some major blunder she was going to carry the night. While she showed no signs of tiring, I realized that I was not tiring either. Our swords were feeding us the energy we needed to keep moving and we were, by the standards of this game, young. Perhaps I could fight to a draw—keep myself alive until dawn. The thought had no more then escaped my mind when I felt a burn across my right side. I hadn't even seen the blow. Had she not been worried about my strength she could have killed me with that one.

A cold sweat broke out along my brow and I realized then that an even colder wind was blowing through the cemetery. The creatures that watched, Sabrina's all, erupted into cheers and shouts. I staggered back and parried wildly at the barrage of blows that followed. She knew she had me and she was moving in for the kill.

I pretended to drop back even father and then as she came on I threw myself at her with abandon. In that moment I could see, from the widening of her eyes, that I had surprised her. Even so my blade missed her by the slimmest of margins. Still, it had been worth it, as she had had to forego a death blow and settle for stabbing me in the thigh. It was deep and I felt my leg buckle and I crashed to the ground. The fall saved me a second time as her blade flashed through the spot I would have been standing in if my leg had not failed me.

And then the cock crowed. It did not seem to me as if we could have been fighting all night, but then this place was outside of time. Sabrina knew the rules as well as I; this fight was, if not a draw, over. I had somehow survived the night.

She lowered her blade and the murderous expression on her face softened. And then as she and her master had all those years ago she started to fade. "Will you still be coming over on Friday?" she asked quickly.

I laughed, relief flooding my very soul. "Of course."

Before she completely faded away I saw her smile, and this time it made it all the way to her eyes.

Milton Keynes UK
Ingram Content Group UK Ltd.
UKHW040858291123
433446UK00003B/60